BROTHERS

David Clerson

BROTHERS

Translated from the French
by Katia Grubisic

QC FICTION

Revision: Peter McCambridge
Proofreading: Riteba McCallum, Elizabeth West
Book design and ebooks: Folio infographie
Cover & logo: YQB MÉDIA
Fiction editor: Peter McCambridge

Copyright © 2013 by Les éditions Héliotrope, Montréal
Originally published under the title *Frères*

Translation Copyright © Katia Grubisic

ISBN 978-177186-086-4 pbk; 978-1-77186-087-1 epub; 978-1-77186-088-8 pdf; 978-1-77186-089-5 mobi/pocket

Legal Deposit, 4th quarter 2016
Bibliothèque et Archives nationales du Québec
Library and Archives Canada

Published by QC Fiction
6977, rue Lacroix
Montréal, Québec H4E 2V4
Telephone: 514 808-8504
QC@QCfiction.com
www.QCfiction.com

QC Fiction is an imprint of Baraka Books.

Printed and bound in Québec

Trade Distribution & Returns
Canada and the United States
Independent Publishers Group
1-800-888-4741 (IPG1);
orders@ipgbook.com

Société de développement des entreprises culturelles
Québec

We acknowledge the support from the Société de développement des entreprises culturelles (SODEC) and the Government of Quebec tax credit for book publishing administered by SODEC.

Financé par le gouvernement du Canada
Funded by the Government of Canada | Canada

We acknowledge the financial support of the Government of Canada through the National Translation Program for Book Publishing, an initiative of the Roadmap for Canada's Official Languages 2013-2018: Education, Immigration, Communities, for our translation activities.

Contents

PART I

The Father

THEY PUSHED THROUGH THE BEATING WINGS and squawks, dozens of birds flapping around them. Their feet sank into the muck. The brine filled their noses, and the smell of muddy water, stagnant and swampy. The first boy, who was missing an arm, walked uncertainly, as if his missing limb pulled him off balance. The second boy followed a few metres behind, his stumpy arms too short for his body. Both had water to the waist, and sweat poured down their faces, faces so similar, their dark eyes, the look of strange, primitive gods.

They had never ventured this far into the salt marsh. But that day, the gulls and the cormorants had gathered there by the hundreds, shrieking, flapping their wings, snapping their beaks. Two turkey vultures soared overhead. The scavengers had not come for nothing: last night's storm must have washed something up on the marshy shores. It had been the younger brother's idea to go exploring. The older brother had agreed, without admitting that he was afraid the tide might surprise them in the marsh. But now he walked ahead, pushing aside the tall grass with his lone arm, and he was the first to see the eye, revealed as the boys' approach scattered the birds that were busy picking at it.

It was the eye of a monster, come from worlds unknown to the two brothers, some abyss swarming with creatures in a universe that was not theirs. Around its soft body, long whitish tentacles floated on the marsh, rotting. Suckers opened and closed like eyes or a row of toothless mouths. The two brothers stared silently, the younger nudging closer to the older brother, standing by his side, where his missing arm should have been. Above them, birds had gathered, circling and shrieking, hiding the sun, impatient to return to their feast. In the shadows, despite the oozing tear of blood, the dead eye of the beast seemed to stare at the two broth-

12

ers. "It's a sign," the younger brother said. "This isn't for nothing. Our father, that dog of a father, also came from the sea."

Back at home, they didn't tell their mother, who was busy cooking a goat stew. In any case, they knew that soon there would be nothing left, that their monster would disappear, polished off by gulls and other seabirds by day, and by night by rats, voracious otters, feral dogs, and day and night by hordes of insects winged or crawling that would dig into the body, burrowing into its flesh as if digging a bottomless den, leaving nothing: no trace, no proof of its existence.

They didn't tell their mother, they didn't know if she would have believed them, but they knew that the beast was from the Great Tide she told them about, the ocean, that infinite expanse of surging black water, unpredictable and menacing, that opened up before them, sealing off their world, and where, she said, lived gruesome, gargantuan creatures, two-headed fish, turtles with shells as big as islands, whales with mouths so large they could consume entire cities. They didn't tell their mother, to whom they spoke less as they grew older, still boys but becoming men, independent, and she now seldom left the grey clapboard house. She was going blind, still able to feed her goats, gather the plants that grew in the fields and the seaweed the tides dragged to shore, but she couldn't see her sons running in the distant hills beyond the marsh, where they could feel the wind push against their bodies, covering them in droplets of salt water from the ocean.

They were growing up, and she had missed it somehow, she who had borne them so late, at an age beyond motherhood, her weathered body, her skin dry, wrinkled and a little loose, returning for them to the vigour of youth. Each night before bed, as in their childhood, she still told them stories, old, disturbing stories, of all the evils wrought by the ocean, the ocean that one day had washed up their dog of a father. He had arrived in a rowboat, she sometimes said, or sometimes it was an old sloop, or perhaps he had been tossed on the shore after a storm, a sire passing through, his lore changing over time and according to the old woman's mood.

Sitting around their goat stew, the two brothers thought about their father, their father who had led a dog's life, a savage life of grunts and yelps under the moon, the kind of life you had to fight for. Where he came from, there was only danger, only gigantic, tentacular creatures: things to fear, to bite, or to kill, things that meant knowing how to bare your teeth. And things too that didn't seem that strange to the two brothers, these deformed boys, children of the valley of Hinnom, which the older brother, that day, associated with the thing they had seen in the marsh, with its eye, and with what he had glimpsed: surreal, hostile worlds—familiar, he thought, to his dog of a father—worlds of darkness and brutality, untamed worlds, unleashed.

"It's a sign," his brother had said, seeing the dead beast in the marsh, and the older brother had believed him, as if his brother, who had to bend so low to the ground to gather curious fossilized shells, snake skins or unusually coloured stones with his atrophied arms, better understood the order of things. The older brother had believed him because he didn't like to doubt, especially those he loved.

Sometimes he and his brother walked for a few hours across the fields to the neighbouring village to trade objects they found on the shore for honey or smoked herring. This was their only contact with the outside world, contact their mother didn't like but tolerated, since, with her old legs and failing eyesight, she could no longer go herself. "Come back soon," she had told them the first few times, and they could feel the knot in her stomach, as if she was afraid of never seeing them again, though now they often left without her knowing they were gone, and she went entire days without seeing them while they explored the coastline or the nearby fields, or risked a quick swim in the freezing, fearsome black water of the Great Tide. She spent her days shuffling back and forth between their grey clapboard house and the goat pen, repeating the same movements she had done a hundred times before, her eyes open but her sight failing, telling herself over and over the same stories she once told her children before bed, and which filled their dreams.

What most drew the two brothers to the neighbouring village were the children they had come across one day, standing deep in a muddy pond, whom they had named the leech-boys.

"What are you doing?"

"We're fishing for leeches."

"What for?"

"To sell them: they say they suck out bad blood."

The children were thin and rangy, with long, salt-tangled hair and skin darkened by the sun. They laughed with all their rotten teeth, the children of fishermen, who spent their days in the plains and hills while their fathers were at sea. The two brothers didn't like them, but kept coming to see them, perhaps to confront their vision of the world, or out of an unhealthy attraction, part curiosity, part disgust.

One day, pointing at the older brother's missing arm, one of the leech-boys asked,

"Why are you like that?"

"It's because of our mother."

"What does that mean, 'because of our mother'?"

"She cut my arm off so that my brother could be born."

"That's not true, that's impossible."

"It's true. She told me herself."

The older brother stared at the leech-boy, a tall angular kid who was missing a tooth, he stared at him and hated him with a hatred that wracked his entire body, from his head to his feet, his brain, his guts.

He spat on the ground. "That's how it is. You wouldn't understand." And he turned and left with his brother. They walked in silence through the field and both of them felt a dumb, screeching rage welling up in their throat, a rage that would not be spent that day, but which they would hold in their bellies for a long time.

They had come into the world on the same day, but only the older brother was born of their mother. That's what she had told him, in the same tone she used for her bedtime stories.

"I love you more than anything, but the world is a cruel place, too cruel to be faced alone. Soon I won't have anything to give you, and there's nothing to be had from your father. That's why I've given you a brother: you'll always be able to count on him, and only him.

"The day you were born, I took you, I came outside, and I laid you on a wide, flat stone, right here, in the garden. You were beautiful, all pink and wrinkled. I leaned over you and I kissed your forehead softly, I told you that I loved you, that everything I did was for your own good, then I hummed old songs my mother had taught me, and which her mother had taught her, songs with a little bit of magic, in a forgotten language—some know the words, but no one knows the meaning—and you listened to me, with your beautiful newborn eyes wide open, as if you found my songs beautiful.

"That day, I remember, the sea had dragged a drizzle over the hills, and then the sun had come out, a glorious summer sun. You were lying on the stone. You looked at me with your big black eyes and I was crying and singing. I took a knife with a sharp blade, I held your left arm, and I cut it off, my eyes closed, still singing. I will never forget your screams, but I knew what I was doing, I knew the ritual: it gives life, erases solitude, and I told myself it was for the best, it was the best thing a mother could do. I covered the wound with a paste of herbs and clay to help you heal, and I kissed your forehead again, still singing for you as you cried and screamed in pain. You don't hold it against me, do you? Tell me you could never hold it against me. (The older brother looked at her with his dark eyes, his gaze telling her that he didn't blame her, that he could never hold it against her.) I don't think I could regret what I did..."

She had told him that his brother had been shaped from his severed limb, and born with two stumpy arms, imperfect but attached to a body that was intact, the body of his brother, with whom he loved to run along the shore and in the hills, and who like him had deep, dark eyes, the same eyes they both shared, the same look of brothers.

That same day and the days that followed, his mother told him, she had repeated time-worn gestures, rituals from the dawn of the world, taking care of her little boys, tending to the wound of the older brother and watching the other one grow, and she soon brought them to her breast, like twins born of the same flesh.

That's what his mother had told him, claiming that an arm was not really much of a sacrifice, that it was a gesture of love that had made him stronger by giving him a brother, and he believed her, as he believed every word that came out of her mouth.

There was no room for doubt, for him or for his brother. And they had no doubt when again they came upon the leech-boys in the neighbouring village.

"So, your brother was born out of your arm?" the one who was missing a tooth asked.

The older brother said nothing.

"It's not true," the leech-boy added. "It can't be. I don't know how you can believe that. It's because the old lady, your mother, wants you to think that what came out of her was normal. But it's not true, you're not normal. It must be because she was too old when she had you, or because of who your father was."

The older brother spat in the boy's face, a sticky white glob of phlegm.

The younger brother hit the boy, driving his head into his abdomen.

They left with a few bruises and torn clothing.

On the way home, the older brother squashed beetles, grasshoppers and other bugs they saw. Finding some snails on a rock, he stomped on them with both feet. A grasshopper that landed on his hand was crushed between his fingers.

The two brothers stopped in the shade of a boulder where farmers had thrown the carcasses of animals that had died during a famine. Only bones remained. The brothers spread them over the ground. Around the skull of a steer, the older brother had fanned out a crown of dog, donkey and horse teeth. His brother had planted phalanges, vertebrae and the thin line of radius bones between the ribs of a goat's ribcage, making it look like a monstrous porcupine. They continued arranging the bones, setting the skull of a chicken on the long tibia of a horse's leg, combining two dog skeletons into a single Siamese creature, setting shoulder blades on either side of a cow's pelvis like the wings of a colossal prehistoric insect. Then they lay down among the beasts, one against the other, faces turned to the sky, with the shadows of their bony creations stretched over their bodies.

The wind blew over them, drying the cuts on their knees and elbows. They were quiet, their mouths closed, breathing calmly although their hearts were beating hard in their chests. They were full of fury, but they felt good there, they had found their place with the bone beasts.

That day, they told their mother that they had had a stupid fight over wild raspberries the older brother didn't want to share. The two brothers never spoke again of the fight, or what had caused it. When the leech-boys next saw them, they saw the fierce look in the brothers' eyes and they avoided the subject too.

And the two brothers kept running across the fields so that it sometimes seemed that they were always running, together, for all eternity, with the sound of the waves breaking on the shore, the waves reminding them of their father who had come from the ocean, the father they would have liked to know and love with a deep love, but different from their love for their mother, a more worrisome love, shadowy, like the waters from which he had emerged, a love both sublime and troubling, inexplicable, a love shaped by a taste for risk, by the temptation of forbidden things.

2

ONE NIGHT, when he had fallen asleep thinking of that monster they'd found in the marsh, the older brother saw his dog of a father. He had pushed his enormous head through the open window of the brothers' bedroom. There he was, his mouth hanging open above the bed, with black gums, damp fur and limp ears, a string of drool trailing from his lip. He said nothing. He didn't grunt, or bark, just drooled quietly, and his warm, sticky spittle dripped from his murderous maw, the jaws that looked like they could kill, and it soaked the older brother's bed, wetting his blankets and his mattress.

The older brother opened his eyes. He got up in the dark night. Without looking at his brother, he went to the open window, saw the pitching sea, its waves battering the shore one after the other, relentless. He looked at it and was frightened: there were too many things he couldn't know, he couldn't face the world alone, he needed his mother and his brother.

He heard his brother get up and join him at the window, right behind him, on his left.

"Did you dream it too? Don't worry. You'll see. One day we'll find him."

And the older brother bowed his head in agreement despite the fear that knotted his stomach and rose up into his throat.

3

THE SEA HAD OFFERED UP not only the monster, but all kinds of marvels. The fish they caught off an old pier barnacled in seaweed and desiccated snails sometimes looked peculiar, with bulging eyes, unusually bright colours or surprisingly spherical bodies. Waves, tides and storms also left things behind, the uses of which they could only guess. One night, a fishing boat had washed up, and they liked to sit in its gutted hull and tell each other stories like their mother told them, stories of the fearful far-away, where everything was abnormally large, peopled by beings the brothers dreamed up with dread, fascinated, as if their strangeness were not so different from the strangeness of these two children, malformed, the sons of an old woman and a wild dog.

Sometimes their mother could help them identify their finds and even predict their value, so they could trade them in the neighbouring village. But it was becoming increasingly harder to interest her: she lived locked inside herself, immune to what came from beyond. The wrinkles on her face seemed to furrow more deeply each day. She looked like a character from her own stories, timeless, outside of time and reality, a reality that never failed to catch her sons off guard, and which seemed so often devoid of logic, or functioning according to systems they couldn't begin to guess at.

That day, walking along the shore with their feet in the water, searching the sand and the rocks for crabs or edible shells, the two brothers saw the waves push out an odd arrangement of pieces of wood, its seaweed shroud giving it a mysterious gleam. They couldn't tell what it was, and the undertow dragged it back out to sea every time it seemed about to wash up.

The older brother was charged with retrieving the thing.

"Go, you do it. I can't," his brother had told him.

He walked into the cold water, which soon came to his waist, torn between the idea that this was not his natural environment and that the Great Tide had far too many things to hide. When the water reached his chest, he had the unpleasant sense that the sea was mocking him, that the object he sought was getting farther away as he approached, but turning back to shore, he looked at his brother and he dove. He was doing it for his brother, not wanting to disappoint him.

He swam, kicking his feet, his arm stretched forward, a frozen current running along his body. He couldn't open his eyes in the salt water and in any case preferred to keep them closed, to see nothing of the depths. His hand closed over a viscous plank. He broke the surface, breathing deeply, pulling in his catch, holding it against his stomach. He swam on his back toward the shore. More than once he thought he might open his hand and release what he'd swum out after, that it was better to leave to the sea the things of the sea, but he held on. He swallowed water, coughed, spat, continued to swim. When his feet finally touched the bottom, he walked in the muddy sand and over the slippery stones to the shore to bring their find to his brother.

They huddled by the fire they had lit to warm up while they fished for shells. The younger brother took his knife to scrape the seaweed from the thing they had pulled from the sea, as if he were shaving off a long, scraggly beard. As he worked, he laughed, overjoyed, already happy with their treasure, a high, rolling laugh that wove into the wind that blew off the ocean. Then he showed the thing to his brother, holding it out in front of him in his short arms.

It was a wooden puppet as big as an almost full-grown child, with a roughly hewn head with a nose, two eyes, and a mouth, and a body with articulated arms and legs. It was wonderful. The brothers had never seen anything like it, and the younger brother held it out proudly, still laughing, he couldn't stop laughing. The older brother was warming himself by the fire, laughing too, but he was more reticent, laughing along with his brother, mostly, a laugh that seemed a little worried at this third playmate, which had risen from the ocean.

When they showed it to their mother, she smiled, a lovely, wrinkled smile, then looked away. They ate together in silence. That night, when the time came to go to bed, they set the puppet on a chair in a corner of the room, and their mother told them the story of a solitary man who, unable to have children, had carved one from wood. He loved him like a son, showed him how to walk and speak, taught him the names of plants and stars and everything he knew, but the son left him in search of improbable adventures.

Her two sons fell asleep, and saw themselves sitting on the roof of their house along with their wooden friend, their home suddenly a makeshift boat, with the bedsheets as sails, and the three of them sailed together over the lands of their childhood, now covered in salt water.

4

THE OLDER BROTHER WAS COMING BACK from
drawing water from the well, a task that was difficult for both his brother and his mother. Even
for him, it wasn't easy: the well was in a gully
about a hundred metres from the house, and the
bucket hung heavy at the end of his lone arm.
To counterbalance the weight, he leaned too far
left, tipping over, stumbling.

Nearing the house, he heard laughter, and
saw his brother a bit farther away, on the side
of the grassy hill, foraging in thorny raspberry
bushes with the puppet on his back: he had
gotten in the habit of tying the puppet to his

back with rope, and as the days passed he was seldom without it. He laughed and talked constantly to the puppet, telling it about his mother, his brother, the story of their birth, and especially their dog of a father, who had also come from the sea, and who had sailed—"you know, in a rowboat, made out of wood like your arms, and he saw monsters, and fought them, like you."

The mother paid no attention to the puppet, although she saw it every day, at the table, sitting next to her youngest son, both of them wedged on the same chair. The mother paid less attention to everything, living as if semi-conscious, mumbling unintelligibly, looking more and more like her old goats, who grazed mechanically, waiting to be sacrificed one after the other to feed the family that fed them.

The older brother carried the bucket of water to the house and went alone to the pier to drop his line, without much hope that anything would bite. He was not a very good fisher. It seemed to him that his brother was better at everything, that the advantages of his longer arm were nothing compared to the abilities of his younger brother, who was better with his hands, better at tying knots, at fixing broken objects, at catching big black beetles, running with his head bent forward, almost along the ground. Yet he loved his brother, did not begrudge him anything: he was part of him, his flesh. "I will always be able to count on him and on him only," he sometimes repeated to himself.

He heard him coming, his telltale footsteps quick and lurching. He didn't turn his head, but smiled: he had missed him. "You're smart to be fishing," his brother told him softly. "Our future is out there, our future is the sea." The wind was blowing in their hair. They breathed in the smell of seaweed, of everything that lived and rotted in the ocean: fish, crustaceans, amoebas, sea monsters, scores of creatures dead and alive, beings of every size, infinitesimally small or terrifically big, devouring each other, feeding off each other, the flotsam of their bodies disappearing in the black water that extended everywhere.

"Did you dream last night?" the younger brother asked.

The older brother didn't reply. He couldn't remember his dreams very well anymore.

"I dreamed of the three of us," his brother went on, "you, me and the puppet, riding on our father's back, his long fur, his tongue dangling out of his mouth. He was running fast. We had

33

to hang on to his fur so as not to fall. He jumped into the ocean and we sailed on his back. It was amazing! I wasn't afraid. You know, the three of us, together, we're going to do great things. I'm sure of it."

The older brother wanted to believe him. His bare feet dangled over the pier, his toes curled up. The fishing line floated on the water: nothing was biting. He wanted something else, but didn't know what. He said, apropos of nothing, "Do you want to go to the village tomorrow? I think we can trade that big beetle, the one with the claws almost as big as a crab's. I think we can trade it with the leech-boys."

"That's a great idea, and we can introduce them to the puppet."

The older brother couldn't help but smile, though he wasn't sure that the visit to the village was such a good idea.

5

THEY DIDN'T GO THE NEXT DAY or the day after that, days of heavy rain that all four of them—the two brothers, their mother and the puppet—spent cooped up in the house, drinking hot seaweed tea and boiled goat milk and telling stories. The younger brother talked a lot; his mouth was full of words. When he spoke, the mother's mind seemed to wander, she would get up, stir her spoons in her pots, look out the window with her almost sightless eyes, and sit back down only to stand right back up again. It was "Puppet," as he called him, who had killed the tentacular monster the two brothers had found in the marsh. It was Puppet, too, who had calmed the storm that had ravaged the area a few years earlier. He had attacked its very source, a tremendous seashell he had smashed to still the powerful winds and the devastating waves that poured out of it. That shooting star the two brothers saw one summer night, that was him too: he had tamed a giant firefly—a grotesque, vanished creature—to ride it across the sky.

The older brother liked these stories—they were nice stories—but his mother's silence worried him. His brother seemed to relish the unknown, while she kept it in shadow. It seemed to him that a breach was opening in their universe, and he didn't know if he wanted that.

The next morning, they left early and walked straight to the village, not stopping to stuff themselves full of raspberries, nor, as they often did, to explore a cave hollowed out in the hillside, nor to visit the bone creatures they had built by the boulder.

The leech-boys saw them coming, and ran to meet them in the fields, the grass still wet from the days of rain. Their fishermen fathers' boats bobbed on the horizon, tiny on the ocean.

"What's that?" the oldest boy asked right away.

"This is Puppet."

"What's it for?"

"It's not for anything, it's Puppet."

"Can I see?"

"You can see, but be careful."

The younger brother held out his wooden friend in his short arms. The leech-boys gathered, curious. The younger brother moved one of the puppet's articulated arms. One of the leech-boys wanted to try. "Careful," the younger brother told him. Soon three of the children were moving the puppet's arms and legs, the younger brother holding it in his hands.

"Heh heh... It's funny. Where did it come from?"

"From the sea... From the end of the world."

"What do you want for it?"

"Nothing, it's just to show you."

"What you mean, nothing? You never come with nothing for nothing!"

"I said, it's just to show."

"Let go. At least let us try it."

The younger brother didn't want to let go. Behind him, the older brother shouted, "Let go! Let go! It's not yours!" but they didn't listen. This was something they had never seen and which they would maybe never see again. It was a thousand times better than the dolls their mothers made for the girls. It looked almost alive, and it had come from the ocean.

The puppet torn from his hand, the younger brother plowed, head down, enraged, charging as he had seen a ram charge and beating his pathetic arms in the air to try to take back what had been ripped from him. His brother tried to follow him, still yelling, "Let go! Let go! Give it back!" but he was beaten back by fists and feet. The younger brother struggled. Hands pulled at him from everywhere. It seemed he would never get Puppet free, but suddenly he caught someone's arm in his two hands and bit it, as an animal bites, a shrieking bite that drew blood into his mouth and tore a scream into the valley. Everyone froze suddenly and let go of the puppet, which tumbled to the ground like a stone. Falling, the puppet's arm and neck broke and the head rolled into the dust.

"Never again! Never again!" the oldest leechboy shouted. "We never want to see you here ever again."

They ran off, leaving the brothers in the trampled grass near Puppet's broken body.

"Look at what they've done to you," the younger brother murmured to his wooden friend.

"They broke you, they've mortally wounded you, I think they killed you..." With tears welling up in his eyes, holding Puppet's head in his hands, he looked like a prehistoric gnome, unfit for this world, weak and pitiful. His brother didn't know what to do. Against his thigh, in a leather satchel, he felt the crab-clawed beetle. He took it out and laid it on the puppet's forehead. It looked like an amulet, the insignia of a prophet from another era.

They carried Puppet like a child lost in combat. The younger brother carried the head and the broken arm in his arms; the older brother held the headless body against him, the remaining limbs dangling. Like lepers, they walked over the wet hills under a sky heavy with grey clouds.

They would never go back to the village; they didn't want to go back there, and both of them knew that they were getting ready to go somewhere else, though they didn't yet know when or how.

They stopped by the rock where they had built their bone creatures. They laid the wreckage of Puppet among them and put the beetle back on its forehead. They stayed there for a long time, stretched out among their own, despite the light rain that had started to fall. It was the older brother who finally convinced his brother to leave, "to get home before nightfall... so we don't get sick." They left together, taking with them Puppet's head and broken arm as the only mementos of their friend.

6

DURING THE DAYS THAT FOLLOWED, it started
to rain again, a seasonal rain, heavy and driven
by violent winds. With the windows closed,
the house filled with the smells of everything
that was cooked on the peat stove: warm milk,
seaweed tea, vegetable stews with a few scant
pieces of goat, fish soup with bones that got
stuck in the throat.

Their mother didn't seem to have noticed
Puppet's disappearance, nor did she notice
that a wooden head and arm now rested on her
younger son's bedside table. To tell the truth,
she didn't really seem to notice anything that

changed her days anymore. The older brother helped her around the house, especially with chores that required going outside: the goats, the garden, collecting wild herbs, smoking fish.

The younger brother spent days in bed, almost without sleeping. He no longer talked about Puppet or to Puppet. He who had been so talkative no longer said a word. His mind seemed to be elsewhere. Then, one day, at supper, he said, softly, just loudly enough to be heard: "The monster, the storm, the shooting star... It wasn't Puppet, it was our dog of a father." No one answered or agreed, but that night, the older brother again saw his father's big head over his bed, drooling, and smiling, a slightly scornful smile, and several times during the night he thought he heard his younger brother snicker in his sleep.

The next day, as he was coming home empty-handed from fishing, the older brother saw his brother sitting in a corner, close to the hearth, in the yellow light of the lantern. He was busy working leather and tying ropes. The older brother approached to see what his brother was doing, but turned back: his brother looked fierce, with the defiant air of those whose tasks are too serious to be interrupted for no good reason. He looked like he was flouting life itself.

The older brother went up to bed.

Opening his eyes in the middle of the night, he saw his younger brother bending over him, his eyes shining and wide open, wide awake, smiling broadly and holding in his hands the puppet's arm. He had rigged a harness made of rope and leather, the straps of the prosthesis to be attached to the shoulder.

The older brother sat up in bed. His ears felt like they were full of laughter, as if all night long someone had been laughing next to him.

"Try it," his brother said.

He did as he was told.

"See, it's perfect."

The older brother had a wooden arm dangling from his left shoulder, an articulated arm, but completely still and unable to move.

"There," his brother added. "You see? You're whole, like the moment you were born."

The older brother wasn't sure if he liked this idea. He thought of their mother, heard her say again, "I love you more than anything, but the world is a cruel place, too cruel to be faced alone... That's why I've given you a brother: you'll always be able to count on him, and only him." And he was filled with a feeling unknown

43

to him, a kind of emptiness, an absence, a treacherous solitude that clenched his guts.

In front of him, his brother was still smiling: "Don't worry. It wasn't my idea. It was our dog of a father. It came from him. It came from the sea. He gave me the idea in a dream. This new arm—you'll see, you won't be sorry."

7

SITTING ON THE EDGE OF THE PIER, the older brother looked out at his fishing line, taut between the waves. "The future is the sea," his brother often told him. Together they inspected everything they fished, from common whiting to queer spiny-finned fish. The older brother fished, his wooden arm hanging against his body. Sometimes, he flexed his muscles, as if to make the arm move, but it didn't move. It was foreign, a parasitic limb he would have liked to be rid of, but his brother told him to be patient. "You'll see, trust our dog of a father." The older brother wanted to believe him, he wanted to believe everything his brother told him, and each morning when he got out of bed he hooked his wooden arm to his shoulder.

Up along the shore, the younger brother was collecting shells, hunched over, his head low between the rocks, waves splashing his face. Often, he lifted his head and looked out over the horizon, laughing happily, as if he could see wondrous, astonishing things.

His harvest complete, he went to join his older brother at the end of the pier, both of them sitting side by side, their legs dangling over the edge and their eyes fixed on the horizon, in their nostrils the smell of seaweed, of salt, of the forever sea. Their skin was brown with sun, their cheeks were a little hollow, and they had the long legs of young men, legs that seemed to have grown too fast for their bodies, legs that seemed especially outsized compared to the younger brother's arms, the arms that he often folded over his chest as if to make himself look bigger, as if this way his arms seemed more firm, solid.

The rainy winter had given way to summer, and the two brothers spent less time in the house. They hardly saw their mother during the day, only really at mealtimes, when they ate quickly, in a rush to leave, faced with this mother who spoke to them as if they weren't there, ghosts of themselves, as if they were the living she could no longer see. She hadn't noticed the older brother's new arm any more than she seemed to notice her children growing older. And her skin was dry, parched, like her eyes, like the inside of her body too, probably. She was slowly turning to dust.

The previous night, after supper, the two brothers had made a big fire on the beach. They had fed it with a few pieces of the piles of wood from one or many wrecks the sea had washed up the day after a storm. "Everything is dead here," the younger brother said. The older brother had already understood that, but he was afraid to leave—to go where? And how?

In his right hand he grabbed his wooden arm and moved it up and down and from right to left, and raised it above his head. His brother came beside him and held the prosthetic limb, and the older brother, his right arm freed, lifted his good arm, and saw in the shadow extending on the shore the towering image of a man with two arms, both raised to the sky, the body of a hero, the stuff of legends, capable of great feats. The two brothers laughed together.

That night, they slept on the beach. In his sleep, the older brother saw his wooden arm running along the sand on the tips of its five fingers, like a crab or a mutant crayfish, and it came to wake him in the night, tugging on his clothes, inviting him to follow as it ran in the ocean.

When the sun woke him at dawn, he thought he heard a dog barking in the distance, and he thought of his dog of a father, sorrowfully for the first time.

8

THEY HAD RETURNED LATE FOR LUNCH, and saw her, their dried-up old mother, seated at the table eating a watery meatless soup, facing two empty chairs. Their chairs. She was talking to herself, to no one, laughing. Serving food and passing the salt and pepper, as if her sons had been sitting in their chairs, and, after she was done eating, rising to clear the table, as if they too had finished their meals. She had not seen them come in, nor did she see them come over to the table. She no longer needed them in order to enjoy their company.

They left again without eating and headed back to the shore. The ocean was still there, humongous, disproportionate. "It would take a miracle for us to be able to leave," said the older brother. His brother smiled wordlessly and led him to the saltpans and the adjacent marshes, to collect as much driftwood as possible. They struggled to carry it back to the rickety fishing boat with the broken hull. They gathered wood all day and in the days that followed, until the younger brother said it was enough.

And they began their task, this monumental undertaking. They would take as much time as they needed. Mimicking as best they could the men they had seen repairing fishing boats in the neighbouring village, they replaced the wreck's rotten wood, nailed planks where the frame was broken and made the boat watertight with a mixture of clay and marsh reeds. They tried many times, trying and failing, often believing they would never succeed, and they took as much time as they needed. It was a big undertaking and they wanted it to be perfect, under the direction of the younger brother, who was amazed at each plank the sea brought them, and which could be of use. They worked as they had played for so long on the sand and in the surrounding hills and plains: laughing, sometimes, but solemnly, as if each movement would leave its mark on the world to come. They worked without doubting their task in the least, but also without ever speaking of the moment they would leave, unsettling but inevitable. Neither had ever sailed, they were awkward swimmers, and increasingly the older brother would wake in the night, nauseated, as if waking after a shipwreck.

Already the boat was seaworthy: one sunny morning, under an almost too-clear sky, they had let it float out, at the end of a rope stretched out from the shore to prevent the ocean snatching it from them. Still they tinkered, adorning it with shells, old dried-out starfish, sea-urchin necklaces. They laid down two straw mattresses. Large jute sacks sewn together would be their sails. The sea had brought them a tall oar, which would be difficult to handle, even together.

Every night, they dragged the boat along the shore to hide it in the marsh, concealing it without quite knowing from whom or from what. One morning, a heron had made a nest in it, and the bird flew off as the brothers arrived. The older brother wondered whether there might be even bigger birds somewhere out on the ocean, with even longer necks, eating fatter frogs, able to peck out the eyes of sea monsters with their beaks. The younger replied that he had seen one once, in a dream, but their dog of a father had leaped at it and sliced its throat with his teeth.

They worried about their supplies, but they could hardly deprive their mother of her scanty stores of salted meat. Her meals were already meagre, her goats underfed, her garden overgrown.

When they weren't working on the boat, the two brothers spent most of their time fishing or collecting shellfish, doing their best to make sure the three of them had enough to eat. Their mother cooked what they brought her, without thanking them, as if it went without saying. If she were by herself, they thought, she would have enough. She ate so little, she needed so little meat and milk to feed her withered body.

One day, the two brothers saw that a goat had escaped from its pen and come into the house. There it stayed, their old mother putting up with it, feeding and milking it.

9

IT WAS ON A FOGGY MORNING that the miracle they were waiting for took place, the two brothers sitting on the edge of the pier in the thick fog. Something was caught on the older brother's line, something heavy that he struggled to reel in. It was a big catch he didn't want to lose, maybe something rare. The older brother panted as he brought in his line. The moist air filled his throat and his lungs were screaming, blood pounding in his temples. His brother encouraged him silently, kneeling on the edge of the pier, his head dangling over the edge, peering into the fog, waiting to see what they had caught.

The older brother didn't think he would make it. He would've needed two arms, but when he pulled his shoulders back, his wooden arm shook ridiculously in the air. He wasn't strong enough. "I need you," he told his brother, who came to sit against him, between his legs, back to chest. He hung on to the fishing line with his short arms and they pulled it together, a mismatched, three-armed being.

They heard the thing lift out of the water, saw its shadow rise in the fog, then the beast appeared before them at the edge of the pier, its fur soaked, its maw open and its tongue hanging out. They heaved it onto the pier and came closer, both kneeling, and they thought it looked majestic, this dead dog, this drowned dog. It wasn't their dog of a father, nothing that big or strong, but it was exceptional, a whisper of him. A drowned dog, come from who knew where. A drowned dog fished out of the ocean. A dog upon which each boy laid his head and ear against the black, wet fur, almost believing they could hear the heart beating in the animal's chest, a heart that had beat elsewhere, far away, where they would soon travel, a heart that told them to leave.

The younger brother raised his head and looked at his brother, smiling. "It's a gift from our father. It's all we were missing."

10

LATER, UNDER THE AFTERNOON SUN, they opened its belly with a knife—the same perhaps that had been used to cut off the older brother's arm so that his brother could come into the world. They removed the heart, the lungs, liver, spleen and guts, throwing them to the crabs and crayfish. They emptied the carcass entirely, without complaining, despite the revolting smell. In a cloud of flies, they found decomposing fish flesh in its digestive system, the bones of small mammals—mice or shrews—and seaweed, all the random things the dog had eaten. With the knife, they removed its pelt, washing it carefully.

Then they laid it over the garden fence in the sun.

When the pelt was dry, they tanned it and made it into a tunic. The snout became a cowl with ears, and the paws could be slipped on like gloves.

The older brother tried it on and he was no longer afraid. It fit perfectly. His wooden arm, under the pelt, seemed almost alive. Wearing the skin, he wanted to run through the fields, to hunt lost cats and moorhens, to grunt and to bark. He and his brother spent the day in the fields and hills, running and laughing. "My dog of a brother! My dog of a brother!" the younger brother cried, his voice ringing with happiness.

At nightfall, the older brother even hazarded a bark.

During the days that followed, they began to set aside stores in anticipation of their departure. From their mother they took only smoked herring and a single pot of cream. One night they walked in the moonlight to the neighbouring village, the older brother wearing his pelt and the younger brother carrying a jute bag on his back. They broke into the communal storehouse and took nice round cheeses and big hunks of salted meat. Behind the house where one of the leech-boys lived, they jumped the fence into the chicken coop and took three live chickens to accompany them on their adventures.

Then they stole away before dawn, unseen and unheard.

They returned home shortly after sunrise. That day, they checked that their boat was watertight and packed their store of food as well as a big barrel of water, and that night they ate in silence with their mother.

She talked as usual, mumbling about her goats, the winter cold, the stormy days, the taste of fish (she preferred meat), and the perils of the sea, with its flesh-eating monsters and its lethal vastness.

The brothers said nothing.

The next morning, they left at daybreak without saying goodbye to their mother, who would not hold it against them, but with a knot in their stomachs and a vague nausea hovering in their throats. "Come back soon. Come back soon," they could hear her repeating.

As they neared their boat, the older brother noticed a figurehead at the front of the craft: the head of Puppet, which his brother had mounted early that morning, draping long strands of seaweed into a beard that would flow in the wind.

The older brother saw the beauty of the thing and his eyes filled with tears.

They pulled the boat out of the marsh and climbed aboard with their three chickens, their stores of food, their too-long oar and a few blankets. A light wind blew on the coast. They hoisted the sail and set out to sea.

11

DRESSED IN HIS PELT, the older brother steered the boat: a dog of a brother to lead them to their dog of a father.

The first days, it took a long time to get away from the shore. Not by choice, but because the wind kept them there, or they didn't know how to handle their sail, to make the boat go where they would have wanted. Instead, they followed the coast, in a direction they had never been, not toward the marshes and the neighbouring village, but out to where the coastline fell away steeply, with cliffs sliced by creeks and a multitude of shrieking birds soaring above.

At night, they slept little, fearing that the wind might push them back to shore and run their boat aground.

Day and night, they worked to plug the leaks that sprang up between the boards with some of the clay they had thought to bring.

On the fourth day, they saw fleecy beasts with long, oval bodies swimming around a rock.

On the fifth day, a strong wind blew them away from shore, and a few hours later they had lost sight of land.

On the sixth day, one of their chickens died, and they threw it overboard. The other two hadn't laid any eggs so far. They considered eating them, but didn't dare, for fear of setting fire to the boat.

On the seventh day, strong waves broke against the boat and many times they thought they would capsize. Both were overcome by seasickness.

On the eighth day, they cleaned their vomit-splattered blankets and clothes as best they could, and threw the last two chickens, which had not survived the night, overboard.

On the ninth day, they caught sight of a colossal beast in the distance, its body black and smooth as stone, diving under the water to resurface immediately, tirelessly, and they were afraid.

It rained all the tenth day, the next night, and the eleventh day, and, using pans, they had to constantly bail out the water that threatened to flood their boat.

On the twelfth day, the younger brother ran a fever.

On the thirteenth day, it got worse.

On the fourteenth day, he didn't get up, delirious in his sleep, rambling about fish-women and crayfish-men, about dogs drowned by their masters.

On the fifteenth day, the older brother spotted a black line, barely visible on the horizon: the coastline. He told himself they were nearing their goal, but he wondered how many days it would take them, at the mercy of the winds, to reach the shore. Their store of food was running low. It occurred to him that they had stupidly left behind their fishing rods, but what worried him more was their dwindling supply of water, which they hadn't bothered refilling during the storm.

On the sixteenth day, when he woke, the older brother realized that it was the first time since their departure that he had dreamed about their dog of a father. He had seen him swimming underwater, grazing fish with bristly fins, others with long, eel-like bodies, kelp caught in his fur. He had called to him from the boat, first shouting as if he knew his name, and barking, but his father didn't hear.

On the seventeenth day, the older brother saw a stormy sky cover the horizon and he worried about his brother. He gave him water, thinking that at least the storm would allow him to replenish his supply of water, and he continued to steer without losing sight of land, but without being able to get closer, battling strong, faithless winds he didn't know how to harness. The storm caught up to them at the end of the day. A brief, brutal storm that tore his sails. After the thunderstorm, he removed his brother's soaked clothes and wrapped him in blankets, as in a shroud.

The next day—the eighteenth—he let himself drift, unable to do anything else. He gnawed at a piece of salted meat, his last. He didn't even try to make his brother eat, although he hadn't eaten in days. The sky heralded other storms.

On the nineteenth day, he saw that the wind had pushed them toward the coast, beyond which he guessed at unknown landscapes peopled by extraordinary beasts. He thought again about his dog of a father. He yearned to find him, and risked a pathetic yelp, alone in his boat with his sleeping brother, who was still delirious, muttering indistinct, barbaric words, like an ancient tongue doomed to disappear. At the end of the day, looking at the shore, the older brother understood that he had failed: these were the same cliffs he had seen at the start of his trip, a few leagues from his grey clapboard house. During these many days at sea, unlike anything he might have dreamed, he had not strayed far, navigating haphazardly, and the winds, deceitful, ungrateful and unpredictable, had brought him back.

He cursed the sea, he cursed his brother, he cursed his dog of a father. He thought of his mother, alone with her goat. He imagined her in her boundless solitude; he should never have abandoned her. In his heart, he knew he no longer had any affection for his brother, only a feeling of failure, emptiness mixed with disgust. Thunder rumbled and fat drops of rain fell on his body. Sheltered beneath shreds of the jute sail, he waited, shivering for hours, biting down on ropes in impotent rage, and whimpering, wretched little barks. The storm was violent, the strongest he had encountered so far. During the worst of it, he had to hang on to his mast so that he wouldn't be swept away. More than once, waves crashed over the boat. Vomit swelled high in his throat. He thought he would retch his insides out, expel what little writhed in his empty stomach, but all that came out was a thin string of translucent saliva. At dawn, the storm passed and the older brother fell asleep, exhausted. His brother visited him in a dream, hanging on to him with his crayfish arms, and croaked angrily, "Today, you abandoned me." And the older brother thought that it was true, that night he had abandoned his brother to the storm, he had covered himself without a thought for him.

On the twentieth day, he was alone in the boat. His barrel of water and his too-long oar had washed overboard. He walked around the boat like a drunk, trying to forget that his brother was no longer there. All he had left was the figurehead at the bow, still draped with two or three strings of seaweed beard, as persistent as anemones clinging to a rock. The storm had given way to a burning sun. The older brother's mouth was gritty; he was empty and dry. He lay down alone in the bottom of his miserable boat, clothed in his dog pelt, his wooden arm hanging miserably from his shoulder. The boat floated aimlessly. Lying on the boards, the older brother was sweating, and his sweat drenched the pelt, already soaked with salt water. He was hot, he was cold, he tried not to think of his brother, but beneath his closed eyelids he could see him, carried away by a wave at the height of the storm, his miserable arms beating the air before disappearing into the ocean.

The older brother opened his eyes. The sun was still there, blinding, taking up all the room, shimmering on the fur of his dog pelt and on the puddles of water in the bottom of the boat. He saw the sun and he shivered, he was terribly cold, a lonely cold, a cold that seized his body and finished dragging him toward a darkness he believed was eternal.

PART II

A Dog's Life

12

HE WOKE UP ON WET STRAW that smelled like animal, and realized he was hungry. On his hands and knees, he crawled out of the dog-house where he had slept, using his wooden arm for support. As he crawled, he felt a leather collar around his neck, and noticed that a chain was attached to it, restricting his movements.

Outside the doghouse, on the dirt floor, he sniffed, listened, and looked around: a house, the noise of children playing somewhere, livestock in a yellowed pasture. A few metres away, a grey dog, a female, gnawed a bone with a few pieces of still-bloody meat.

The brother moved closer, growling, starving. The bitch raised her head. He growled again, and she moved away. He went over to the bone, dragged it toward him, and chewed at it hungrily. The other dog looked at him from a distance, her ears flattened.

When he finished his meal, the brother, exhausted, returned to his doghouse. He didn't want to think about the past or the future: he only wanted to sleep.

When he awoke, vague memories came back to him: people rescuing him from the bottom of his boat, dumping him in a wheelbarrow, and pushing him over winding roads.

He didn't know if he should feel lucky to have survived, but in the end it didn't matter much: he wasn't so unhappy here, comfortable in his doghouse. Life seemed organized, predictable: he had nothing to fear. He stretched his aching limbs. Outside, fat flies buzzed close to the ground, weighed down by the summer heat. He poked his head out into the sun, where he was happy to find a bowl of lukewarm water and lapped from it thirstily. He stretched out, his head outside the doghouse, and shocked himself by licking a scratch, probably a wound sustained during the storm. Then he fell back asleep.

It was the smell of food that woke him. He saw a fat woman emptying a bucket of bones and table scraps a few metres from his doghouse, and he stood up and ran toward her, a little awkward on four legs. "Awake at last! It's about time," she said. He looked at her. She seemed to be waiting for something. He thought it wise to bark; she seemed satisfied: "Good boy. I have a feeling you and I are going to get along." And she left.

The brother gnawed at the bones for a long time, wagging his tail. The grey dog was looking at him, sitting apart. When he had finished his meal, he heard her come over to eat his leftovers. She had a nice pelt, he thought; next time, he would try to leave her a little more meat.

Then he went to sleep, again: his recent ordeal had exhausted him.

At night, he was awakened by howls. Wolves, he thought, or coyotes. He fell back into a nervous sleep.

The next day, in front of the doghouse, he saw the fat woman and six round, red-faced children wearing horizontally striped shirts. Piglets, he thought to himself, pig-children. "You see, kids, he's a good dog. You, come here. Do you think you could explain what you were doing on that boat?

That doesn't really happen, a dog on a boat. Come on, don't be afraid, come..." He came closer. "See how nice he is. Who wants to give him a bone?"

"I do! I do!" the children cried in unison.

The oldest and roundest of the children handed him a bone, the biggest he had ever seen in his bitch of a life. The boy held it out with a malicious smile, taunting him with a little squealing sound. The brother came closer. The boy inched back. The brother moved closer. The boy moved back again, still squealing. The brother got to the end of his chain and growled. It made the children laugh, but the fat woman came up and kicked him in the ribs. He retreated, stung. "Growl all you want, but not at the children!" He understood her words, but he was mesmerized by the bone; he wanted the bone very badly. Still, he dropped his head, chastened. "Good! You can give him the bone," she told her oldest son. The child approached and tossed the bone a couple of metres away from the older brother, who yanked on his chain but couldn't reach it. Finally, the fat woman shoved the bone at him with her foot. He grabbed it and crawled back through the dust to his doghouse.

In the days that followed, he was gentler and more understanding with the children, and the fat woman almost never kicked him. Still, he was taken aback when the children decided to take him for a walk. Did they really like him? He didn't believe it. He was their toy, at the mercy of their whims, a poorly tamed beast held captive by a children's circus.

There were five or six of them, walking slowly under the sun, waddling like little pigs, but too clean, as if they had given up rolling in the mud. Their faces were red and fat. The brother followed along on his four legs, increasingly accustomed to using the fourth normally, like a cripple learning to walk again.

The day was unbearably hot. The children wore straw hats to protect themselves from the sun. They walked unevenly, like drunks, weaving left and right and turning on themselves in their striped shirts, like they took nothing seriously, always with slightly stupid smiles on their faces. The oldest squealed away at the head of the pack, flies landing on his forehead.

They led the older brother to a large coastal village, almost a town, with paved streets the likes of which he had never seen. He was used to the muddy, trash-lined roads in the village where the leech-boys lived.

Along the way, dogs barked their heads off at him, running toward him, jerking at the end of their leashes; all sorts of canines with bone-crushing jaws: short, aggressive bulldogs, hateful basset hounds, tall, scraggy bouviers with droopy lips. The brother could smell their hatred and reacted to their provocations, growling or barking back, but each time the children yanked his leash to shut him up his collar squeezed his throat and he dropped his head in silence, a thin string of saliva seething between his teeth.

Now and then, the fattest of the children would amuse himself by stabbing a sharp stick into his back, and when they sat on the dock, sharing fat chunks of sausage, he even poked him under the eye because he had been so bold as to beg for his share.

Only when they were done eating did they flick him the casings, which he ate without complaint. The heat of the sun on the children's red faces made them sweat and covered them in a varnished sheen.

Shortly before they left the village, they passed a heap of wooden planks piled at the edge of the port. The brother recognized the split wood of his boat, of his and his brother's masterpiece, and he looked at it as one looks at the remnants of an era better left behind without regret. At the top of the stack stood the head of Puppet, with a few last strands of seaweed still attached to his chin. Someone had painted the wooden face black and white, disfigured it, with a wide, smiling mouth, toothy and laughing. The work of a child, the brother thought, or a simpleton.

Seeing Puppet's grin at the top of the heap, the pig-children laughed too.

13

A FEW DAYS LATER, as he was circling the grey dog in the humid heat of the summer afternoon, the brother suddenly wanted to smell her hindquarters, and she quickly also smelled his. Seeing them, the children writhed with strangled laughter. "The world is a cruel place," the brother thought, his muscles tensed, and he roared inside.

On his four legs, he felt complete, more sure of himself than ever. He began to find his fangs, acquiring a taste for biting. He was no longer afraid when he heard coyotes and wolves howl in the night. He was growing more ferocious, with the ferocity of an adult male, as he had so often imagined his father.

He no longer thought of his brother, or very little. He no longer thought of his past life, a life spent in fear, being small in the world, crushed by the weight of the sky and the enormity of the ocean.

Sometimes, the children untied him and let him run free in the fields. He chased groundhogs and hares, breaking their necks with a single bite.

"The world is a cruel place," his mother had told him. He remembered, but he was no longer afraid to face it alone. At night, he dreamed of himself only as an animal, and in his sleep he chased over never-ending plains, chasing creatures that grew larger every night, bounding over red, blood-soaked earth.

He had learned to obey his masters, but he also noticed every beat of the pulse in their jugular veins.

One night, with a hard heat in the pit of his belly, he mounted the grey bitch, imitating the ram he had seen when villagers brought the animal to inseminate his mother's goats.

He didn't linger, retreating to his doghouse, the taste of disgust in his mouth: he pictured his dog of a father mounting his mother like that, and all the suffering of his birth washed over him, the incomprehension of what he was. Alone in his doghouse, an irrational numbness filled his left arm, his wooden arm, a numbness that marked hours of insomnia while an offshore wind blew wet over the fields and up to his doghouse.

14

HE FELL ASLEEP TO THE REPULSIVE IMAGE of his dog of a father lying on top of his mother, and his father, that stray dog, came to him again in his sleep, the wide head slipping through the doghouse door, invading it, enormous, taking up all the space. His breath turned the air sour, his gums were wet and slimy, and his snout sniffed at the brother, recognizing him as his own, his own line, and he was satisfied, proud of his dog of a son.

The next night, when he saw the grey dog, the brother sniffed her ass and mounted her again, this time with true pleasure. They lay together for a long time, their warm bodies entwined on the bedding of his doghouse, and they found themselves speaking. Like him, she was the daughter of a dog of a father, a passing male that had impregnated her mother. She had looked for him for years, and had found him, but it had gotten her nowhere, she had become a bitch in his image, a dog turned wild, often injured and starving. She had been beaten and had learned to fight, before ending up here, in this doghouse, finding the brother, his smell and hers, the beating of their hearts, their breath on each other, and the feeling of invincibility that would lead them somewhere they didn't yet know.

In the days that followed, they shared their meals, chewing the same bones together. Wrapped around each other, they slept in the same doghouse. "Look at the lovebirds," the piglets goaded them. And they were right: they made a good couple, he in spite of his worn pelt, and she despite being so thin, her body worn out by flight and hunger.

The brother liked to feel her next to him. He found a proximity he hadn't known for a long time, and it brought him back to childhood, reminding him of his brother walking by his side like a part of him he never thought he would lose. He remembered and, despite the grey dog close to him, he felt alone again, he felt the absence of his brother, and a wave of nausea rose from his stomach as he remembered that he had abandoned him. Then he turned to his companion, licking her snout, huddling against her and thinking to himself that maybe he loved her. It was a new feeling for him, different than what he had felt for his mother or his brother, different than the uncertain affection he sometimes felt for his dog of a father, yet similar, a feeling of unreasonable attachment, with no real cause, which neither blood nor desire were enough to explain. A feeling he wished could last forever, something sacred, as his mother and his brother had been.

They rolled around together in the sand or on the bedding, tussled gently over a bone, told each other stories of their escapades—his sea odyssey, the unfamiliar lands she had crossed— but the brother told himself that it wouldn't last, and sometimes he saw in her eye a disquieting glimmer that led him to believe that she didn't hold out much hope either that they would love each other for long.

15

THEY SAW IT ARRIVE IN A WHEELED CAGE pulled by an old donkey, driven by a small, dry man. They saw it arrive and it was prodigious, a big, black thing, muscular, with tiny, deep-set eyes, nearly invisible, lodged in a head that was all jaw, all teeth. It was a pure and primeval breed, a monstrous canine, a caged dog that no one wanted to set free.

The brother couldn't help but think back to the monster he and his brother had found dead in the high marsh grass. The dog wasn't as big, nor surprising, but he suspected it could be as aggressive. This was a creature he would have preferred to encounter defanged, harmless, a simple hunk of flesh left to the scavengers, but the animal was very much alive, and he could only surmise it had bad intentions.

It had arrived a few days earlier and had made its way through the village before coming there with the piglets and their sow of a mother. The dog had been admired in the village square, not far from the dock, always caged, and then, in exchange for cash or crates of smoked herring or stacks of wheat, it had been mated with almost every bitch in the village in the hope of producing combative bastards, big guard dogs to keep away foxes and thieves, even if many of the mothers would die whelping.

The ritual was repeated: each female was brought into the cage; the male dominated her and mounted her as his masters watched. Then she was taken quickly from the cage for fear that, in a rage, the dog might kill her.

Now it was the grey dog's turn.

She knew what awaited her. The brother, meanwhile, pulled on his chain and barked frantically, powerless, but nobody paid any attention.

The piglets' fat mother, along with the dog's owner, walked toward the grey female. The children watched at a distance, eyes wide in their fat, blood-red faces.

"You'll see, little one, you're going to give us nice pups," said the fat woman as she approached the dog. The grey female bent her head submissively, prepared to be sacrificed. Her mistress held out her hand. The brother barked even louder. The children snickered. Suddenly, the grey dog raised her head and dug her fangs into her mistress's white hand, felt her blood run into her mouth. The scene froze for a moment in the bright afternoon light, then the fat woman backed away, with a long cry of pain, a long, almost animal cry, a sow getting a taste of the slaughterhouse.

In his doghouse, the brother couldn't help but be proud of the grey female, but he suffered with her as a stick came down on her back once, twice, three times, and he heard her whimper, an almost human whimper, in proud, desperate pain. And he wondered how much of his father's blood really ran in his veins, and whether he would have been able to accomplish even a fraction of the exploits his brother had attributed to him: slaying monsters, stopping storms, flying like a flame through the sky.

He saw the injured dog struggling to crawl toward her doghouse, and for the first time since the shipwreck he thought about the day he had awakened in the boat with his brother gone. He felt his throat constrict. He thought of the wave that must have washed over them and taken his brother without him even realizing, without being able to help, he had already probably given in, he had abandoned his younger brother, born of his body, part of him, his flesh, and he decided that he would not abandon the grey bitch like his dog of a father had abandoned his mother.

He remembered his brother's laugh and his words when he spoke of their father: "Don't worry. You'll see, one day, we'll find him." Hopeful words, when there was no more hope. Everything had seemed dead around their grey clapboard house with their mother who was forever dying, but here too there was always death, and everywhere else. Maybe all he had left was the grey female, who, wounded, had retreated to her doghouse. Everything was death, but he wanted to bite. He would do it for her. No one anywhere was waiting for him. She might be all he had.

16

MATING HAD BEEN POSTPONED to the next day. They would take precautions, muzzle and hold the dog so that she would not be able to bite or fight back.

In the dead of night, the brother withdrew his hand from the right paw of his dog pelt. It was bloodless and curled up, like the foot of a dead chicken. He stretched his fingers, felt heat come back into them, brought his hand to his neck and undid his collar. Then he put his hand back in his pelt and went out of his doghouse. He walked to the other doghouse and slipped inside. "How do you feel? Come on, we have to go." Her left ear was mangled and she likely had a broken rib, but, she assured him, she could still run, not as fast as usual, but fast enough for them to be far away by daybreak. The older brother felt tenderly toward her, a human tenderness, he wanted to take her in his arms, but they couldn't wait, he told her, it was time to go.

They went out under the vast starry sky, a universe of possibilities open over their heads, and he remembered standing with his brother before a pond in the middle of the night, watching the reflection of the stars in the water and wanting to dive in, to swim in the infinite sky.

Close to the house, they saw the cage of the sleeping animal, fantasized for an instant about killing it from the outside, sliding spikes between the bars and stabbing it through the heart, but they chose to flee.

Behind the house, the fields opened up. They walked around the barn to avoid being seen and they heard a squeal, a familiar squeal, and above them they saw the fat, round head of the oldest, the fattest and roundest of the piglets, his flesh squeezing out from under his striped shirt. He was sitting in the barn's second-floor window, his legs dangling over the ledge. His face was painted grotesquely, with broad strokes like on

Markham Public Library
Markham Village Branch
LMV - POS 02
6031 Highway 7 E.
Markham, ON L3P 3A7
www.markhampubliclibrary.ca
905-513-7977 ext. 4271

Symphony Account Payment
MV-Overdue Materials
1x   0.00   0.00
MV-Overdue Materials:
1x   0.90   0.90
MV-Overdue Materials:
1x   0.90   0.90
MV-Overdue Materials
1x   0.30   0.30
MV-Overdue Materials
1x   0.30   0.30

Subtotal: 2.40
Total: 2.40

Cash LIB   3.00
Change   0.60

12/11/2017   15:50   a 470
#3337998 /99/23
Receipt #:   4499503
Please take a moment to complete our
customer satisfaction survey.

www.markhampubliclibrary.ca/
UsingTheLibrary/
CustomerSatisfactionSurvey

Markham Public Library
Markham Village Branch
LMV - POS 02
6031 Highway 7 E.
Markham, ON L3P 3A7
www.markhampubliclibrary.ca
905-513-7977 ext. 4271

Symphony Account Payment
                1x   0.00   0.00
MV-Overdue Materials
                1x   0.90   0.90
MV-Overdue Materials
                1x   0.90   0.90
MV-Overdue Materials
                1x   0.30   0.30
MV-Overdue Materials
                1x   0.30   0.30

SubTotal: 2.40
Total: 2.40

Cash LIB   3.00
Change   0.60

12/1/2017   15:50
#2337998 /99/23
Receipt #:   4499903
   Please take a moment to complete our
     customer satisfaction survey.

       www.markhampubliclibrary.ca/
              UsingTheLibrary/
        CustomerSatisfactionSurvey

Puppet's head. "I've been watching you for a long time," he told them. "What do you think you are? Human? You're dogs, with a dog's life." They said nothing, but both looked at him like a piece of throbbing flesh. It would have been so easy to make him bleed. "I know you'd like to leave. You can't keep still. But we're going to tame you!" And he jumped down, falling like a ball to block their way, a stick in his hand.

The two dogs growled. The boy windmilled the stick, laughing and squealing, proud to have trapped them, skipping gleefully around on his two legs, his stick whistling through the air, forcing them to drop their heads to the ground, and they were frightened, stupidly, these supposedly fierce creatures, deferential before a stick, trapped by a child, and they backed away, and the brother in his dog pelt told himself that they must not give in, that he had put on the skin of a predator, that he carried in him the ferocity of the most vicious dogs. His brother had told him that they came from a world of giants, their father's world, his brother had given him the tools of his deliverance.

He lifted his left paw, his wooden paw, which blocked the child's stick as he swung, and he stood straight up, like a man, and like an animal

93

he bit into the fat throat of the child who squealed as he crumpled, a pig's squeal, a squeal that rang out for a long time as they ran across the fields.

The brother spat as he ran to get rid of this new taste in his mouth, the taste of human blood, but it coated his palate and his tongue and it disgusted him.

The grey female, her body racked with pain, was running more slowly than she had hoped.

They stopped. "Did you kill him?" she asked, knowing the answer, the question without reproach but full of fear, a question that signalled the suffering to come. "You're in pain," he said to her, "but we have to continue. We can't let them catch us."

"We won't let them catch us," she promised. And he thought to himself that he loved her.

The fields rose slowly over the hills. The wind blew in from the ocean, and the smell of earth and wheat mingled with salt, seaweed and fish. A smell that was familiar to the brother, the smell of his childhood, a smell he had known for so long before his life as a dog. He ran across the fields and up the hill, although the grey dog was out of breath and had to stop often, and the older brother worried that they couldn't run faster.

The squeals of the slain child had roused the household, and their screams had alerted the village. The brother and the grey dog could hear shouting and barking behind them, and he imagined also the moaning and the weeping.

They didn't know whether they were afraid. They were neither hopeful, nor despaired. They fled as best they could, as the grey dog had so often fled, she who for the first time no longer ran alone.

Their flight under the stars was their honeymoon, a consecration of love that sneered at death.

The female was suffering, and she was so exhausted that they had to stop, a little longer this time. Behind them, a long line of torches advanced across the fields, and they could hear dozens of dogs barking.

"Don't tell me to leave you," the brother said to his companion. He pulled out his right hand and slid it under the grey dog's pelt; there he felt human skin, beaded with sweat, and in her chest he could feel her heart beat.

He made her climb on his back and he ran upright, his gait often faltering, his legs no longer accustomed to holding him upright. The torches got nearer, and the barking nearer still.

They had set a pack of dogs on them, dozens of village dogs. Bulldogs, bassets, bouviers; dogs that, giving chase, woke every animal in the fields: hares, foxes and shrews that now scaled the hills alongside the fleeing lovers. Dogs that ran faster than the brother could run with the grey dog on his back. Dogs that would devour both of them even if they decided to remove their animal skins to become human again.

And there he felt rising in him the feeling that he had not escaped death to die like this. He had already saved his lover from humiliation, but he couldn't save her life, and, rather than die with her, he would avenge her, a terrible vengeance, savage, a vengeance only he and his brother could have imagined.

He would leave her to her death, but he would carry her with him in his vengeance, the revenge of the human heart, driven by an animal rage.

He put her down on the ground. "There's nothing we can do," she told him. He nodded. "Go." He nodded. "You told me you wouldn't leave me."

"I won't leave you."

He took off her pelt. She stood there, naked in the grass, weak and shivering.

He slipped her pelt over his.

"You see, I'm taking you with me."

And he left without looking back, but his chilling, animal howl echoed under the sky. Below, he saw the line of fire split up, one part following him, and the other continuing toward the one he had loved. Dogs barked on both sides.

He ran, howling unabated, howling for himself, howling for the grey dog, howling from his throat and through her mouth, howling so he wouldn't hear her die.

17

HE HAD NEVER LIKED SWIMMING, but he quickly understood that he would escape them by taking to the sea. There, the dogs wouldn't be able to find him, and he swam as he had imagined his father swimming, and as he imagined his brother swimming, snatched up by a wave and swept away into an underwater kingdom where his stubby arms fluttered among the jellyfish.

He swam, caught his breath in a creek, swam again. For days he huddled in a cave until they weren't looking for him anymore, assuming that the hunted animal had managed to run away, never to return.

With his two pelts, he wasn't cold, inhabiting the remains of a dog and a bitch, feeling more than ever like a complete being, albeit a strange one, one of the hermaphrodites that sometimes appeared in his mother's stories.

He ate shells and crabs. He drank rainwater that pooled in a hollow of a stone.

He was not afraid.

As night fell he lay on the beach. The sand was warm. The wind was soft. The brother slept a restorative sleep.

One night, he dreamed that the head of the grey dog had been planted on the end of a spike, a cloud of flies buzzing around her and covering her, blackened, as if charred, while fat, round children, pig-children dressed in stripes, their faces painted white, danced all around, a primitive dance, a death dance, in honour of the queen of flies.

He woke ready to paint the world the shade of nightmares.

18

HE SURFACED IN THE MIDDLE OF THE NIGHT between two boats in the port. He clambered onto the dock and walked into the village. He headed straight for what was left of his boat and took the head of Puppet, the head on which the oldest of the pig-children had painted a face with a wide smile, and he dove back into the sea with the head, swimming around the village so as not to wake the dogs. He crossed back across the fields, running among the fireflies and the crickets, and came to the piglets' house. He heard a dog bark—already replaced, he thought— and ran as fast as he could toward the doghouse, where he saw a big, grey, mangy cocker spaniel, and brought down Puppet's head on the dog's head, shattering its skull without even giving the animal time to whimper, and he dragged the body with him into the doghouse. There he waited a moment, making sure he hadn't woken anyone. Then he went out.

Hidden in the shadows, hugging the wall of the house, he took off his wooden arm and attached Puppet's head, now stained with the spaniel's blood. Then he removed the grey pelt and used it to clothe this new wooden man. He was holding a big marionette: the head with its broad, bloody smile, dressed in a dog pelt. He held it up and it seemed alive in the night. It made him smile, and he laughed noiselessly, as his brother would have laughed. He thought he might keep laughing like that his whole life.

Without delay, and without fear, he burst into the house, slamming the door. He ran up the stairs, letting his laughter seep out of his chest and bounce against the walls. On the second floor, he burst into the bedroom where the piglets' fat mother slept. He saw her standing there in her flowered nightgown, holding a lantern in front of her, her face contorted by terror, and the light of the lantern made his shadow bigger on the wall, the shadow of a creature of the night, a misshapen dog, a two-bodied being, and he laughed again, letting loose a quick bark between two peals of laughter as he brought down his weapon over the sow's head, and she fell, her lantern shattering over her and setting her body aflame.

The brother went out and came across one of the piglets in the hallway. He brought down the smiling head over the child's skull three times, spraying himself with blood, and he pushed into the piglets' bedroom, where those who were left sat terrified in their beds, and Puppet fell upon each of them in a racket of broken bones and children's screams, the brother's pelt and the puppet's covered in blood. At last, the older brother jumped out the window, seeming to float down as air billowed under the grey pelt all around Puppet. He rolled in the dirt, scratching his arms and legs, but paid no attention to his injuries, and he ran and ran while behind him fire engulfed the house.

He ran toward the sea, silently, and dove in, while from the village rose the barking of dogs and the cries of men and women. He swam back toward the port, climbed aboard a sailboat, cast off, and escaped out to sea.

For a long time he watched the blaze burning in the night in the distance. It was a bonfire in honour of the grey dog, with the ghosts of the pig-children dancing in the flames, a celebration of death, and the brother celebrated too, the blood of his victims drying on his skin. He was not alone: he was with the grey dog and Puppet. To his left, where the prosthetic arm once again left a void, he thought he felt his brother.

PART III

Odyssey

19

THE SAILBOAT WAS SMALL AND LIGHT, made of wood, and it glided on the ocean, attended by graceful seagulls and a few cormorants. This craft was much easier to handle than the brothers' rowboat. This time, the older brother headed straight out to the open sea, pushed by fair, warm summer winds.

He had secured Puppet's head to the bow, leaving his figurehead clad in the grey pelt. Often, the wind would fill the pelt, moving the body and limbs. It seemed to dance at the bow, and it made the older brother smile, a fleeting happiness.

There had been a barrel of fresh water in the boat when he set sail, along with a few dry biscuits and some smoked herring. The older brother ate parsimoniously, nearly fasting, and he almost never slept, his eyes wide open over dark circles carved out by a scalpel.

The blood had dried on his face and on the pelt he wore. His skin was tanned by the sun, and hairs were beginning to sprout on his young man's skin. He was not good at handling the sail and had quickly abandoned the idea of hoisting it, simply letting the waves carry his sailboat. He spent the days and nights standing in the bow, behind Puppet dressed in the grey pelt, with the wind blowing over his body and sprinkling droplets of salt water on his skin.

He had placed his prosthetic arm in the bottom of the sailboat. Fine cracks had begun to appear on the wood. It had been the arm of a puppet swept away by the ocean, and also the limb of a strange child, the paw of a dog turned murderous, and the handle of a weapon; most of all it was a present from his brother, a present he didn't know what to do with.

The first days, the older brother passed a few small islands, then, nothing. Fewer and fewer birds travelled with him.

He rarely thought of the past.

He never felt alone.

In the bow, looking out at the ocean's black water, he sometimes thought he was seeing things: giant squids, tritons and sirens swimming in the depths. His kin, he told himself. Monsters like him.

In his rare moments of sleep, he saw himself as a bloodthirsty god, marching over plains of burnt grass covered with cadavers, Puppet in his hand like a mace. He slaughtered women and children, and Puppet laughed, laughed and laughed.

After sailing for several days, despite his frugality, his stores of food were coming to an end, and he fasted in earnest. Always under the sun in the bow of the boat, he sometimes caught himself sleeping standing up. His body thinned out, the body of a wandering saint, with dried blood encrusted in the hollows of his face, and the cruelty of the world in his belly. He kept squinting: the light of the sun seemed threatening.

One morning, opening his eyes, the older brother saw a raven standing on Puppet's head, and he thought he must have passed an island while he was sleeping, that the raven must have come from land nearby. He began to dream of Puppet's home country, a world of wooden beings, a land of war, of bloodless wars, all splinters and wood shards, and the thought pleased him.

It might have been one of his mother's ideas, he thought to himself, not expecting to be thinking about her, and he wondered whether she still talked to them, to him and his brother, every night at supper, if she still warned them against the temptations of the ocean, against that dog of a father that the brothers had wanted to meet despite the fear of sinking into the depths, never to return, into the depths from which the older brother sometimes thought he heard his brother's laugh rising, as if he were at some eternal carnival with the tritons and the sirens.

Maybe the raven perched on Puppet's head heard the laugh too. The bird stood there, its plumage black and glossy, looking at the older brother before turning its head toward the ocean. It must have seen and heard so many things, the older brother thought. "Raven, have you heard my brother's laugh?"

"Caw," the bird said.

The older brother hadn't spoken in a long time, barking, mostly, over the last few months. The sound of his voice startled him. It sounded scratchy. He wanted to hear it again. "Caw? Caw, what?" he asked the raven, who turned its head toward him quizzically, but did not answer.

The next day, clouds filled the sky, growing darker as time passed. The older brother's ribs were sharp under his skin, just above his hollow abdomen. He felt emaciated, his pelt huge and shapeless around him. He was a gaunt animal, a starving old dog lost on an ocean he didn't know the end of, but where he floated without fear, without fearing death, but without wanting it either, without worrying about it.

He was tired. He had a hard time telling sleep from waking. And his brother's laughter trickled up from beneath the waves more and more often, a jellyfish laugh, the laughter of the deep. The older brother's ears were full, and his nose and his mouth. The laugher came into his body and filled his belly and his head, denying his brother's death, as if it had been only a mirage.

Often, the older brother opened his heavy, pasty mouth to ask the raven, who never left him, "Do you hear it too? Do you hear?" The raven didn't answer, not even deigning a simple caw. It hopped along the gunwale, sometimes opening its wings to keep its balance.

The older brother no longer associated his brother's laughter with happiness. He even wondered whether he had ever been right to think he was happy. Sometimes, it sounded snide; more often, he thought the sound seemed unhappy, laughter tinged with suffering, and he associated that suffering with their dog of a father: for him they had left their mother, for him they had set out to sea without knowing how to sail, for him his brother had been swallowed by the ocean, this ocean now echoing with the haunting laughter that rang in the older brother's head, as if to say, "What were we supposed to find, when we found our father?"

The older brother sometimes closed his eyes and saw a wide, black, furry head emerging from the ocean, long strands of seaweed tangled in its fur, drooling over the boat as the older brother had so often seen him drool in his dreams. He had always been that big in his dreams, but the jaw was weaker now, with decayed teeth hanging loosely from rotten gums, and he told himself that he scared him less than before.

When, after many days of grey, rain finally fell on the older brother's face, the water washed the dried blood, which ran into his mouth, and he drank it. The rain also washed his pelt, caked with the blood of the pig-children and their mother, and water mixed with blood pooled in the bottom of the boat. The raven cawed while the rain ran over its feathers. The older brother gathered water in the palm of his hand and wet his face. He threw his head back and drank the rain as it fell from the sky, while the raven ran around in the bottom of the boat, circling around him, cawing.

It rained a long time. As best he could, the older brother made a shelter, pulling the sail tight over the hull. He brought down Puppet from the bow, and took the head with him under the sail. The rain had cleaned the blood off Puppet and wiped away the painted smile. The older brother placed the head in front of him, both of them lying beneath the sail, and he spoke to Puppet as if to an old friend: "Do you remember the first time we saw each other? I pulled you out of the ocean. I did it for my brother. You were covered in seaweed. He had to wash you. Can you hear him laughing? He loved you so much..." Then he pulled the grey dog's pelt over himself, petted it and said: "I loved you as I may never love again, and I avenged your death better than you could have dreamed."

His brother's laughter echoed under the sail in the shelter, and the older brother began to sing a song without words, though words slipped into the tune, words he didn't know, archaic words maybe, or new words created from nothing, devoid of meaning, a tune like his mother used to sing, maybe the same one she had sung on the first day of his life to reassure him while she cut his arm off.

He sang to chase away his brother's laughter, but couldn't. His song rose from his empty stomach, where the laughter had already seeped in, and it filled the sail, mixing with the laughter that quickly drowned out the music. The older brother stopped singing and began to cry, tears streaming from his dry body.

The next day, when morning came, the rain had stopped and the older brother had fallen asleep, covered with the grey pelt, Puppet next to him.

In his dream, he was walking on the ocean as one might walk across a desert, an ocean covered in bodies, a dry sea, not fit for life, and he felt his hunger scream from the pit of his hollow stomach, a screeching voice like his brother's on his angry days, a raging voice that nothing but the taste of blood would appease. And always he heard his brother's laughter, laughter that sneered at death, and the older brother wanted to believe it, dreaming of his brother alive for all time.

At the peak of the afternoon, as the sun began to pierce the clouds, the raven joined him under the sail. The older brother turned to the bird in his sleep and asked, talking in his dream: "Did you hear him laughing?" The raven snapped its beak and answered in its bird's voice, the voice of a ventriloquist in which the older brother thought he heard his own: "Caw. Your brother hasn't laughed in a long time. Your brother is dead, unquestionably dead." Then the older brother woke, staring into the empty eyes of the silent bird. How he hated this bird of ill omen. He grabbed it suddenly with his hand, brought it quickly to his mouth, bit into its throat and felt blood run over his tongue, and twisted its body to break the neck. Then he came out from beneath the sail, knelt under the sun, plucked his victim with his teeth, and ate the body raw before throwing the remains overboard.

He got up and looked out over the horizon and saw a dark shape swimming under the surface, a ghastly shape swimming away from him. He knew it: it was his father. He had set sail for his father. He had always been heading here. His brother had died wanting to find their father;

if his brother was dead now, it was because his father had killed him.

And now, the older brother was going to kill his dog of a father.

20

THE OLDER BROTHER HAD ONCE again made Puppet the sailboat's figurehead. The boat had become a battleship, launched in memory of his younger brother with the atrophied arms.

He had replaced the wooden arm on his left shoulder, and pulled the grey pelt over his own. They were weapons of war, offered up by those he had loved, the weapons of a warrior god with demented eyes.

He fastened his sail to the mast, and barked: the hunt was on.

It wasn't long before he spotted a large shadow swimming underwater off in the distance, and he kept his eyes hooked in it, the eyes of a sleep-walker tracking a nightmare.

On the first day of the hunt, he couldn't get close to the beast.

On the second day, he even thought he might lose sight of it.

On the third day, it seemed closer, and he thought it might have been swimming more slowly.

On the fourth day, he heard his mother's voice. "The world is a cruel place, too cruel to be faced alone." "I'm not alone," he replied. "I have the bitch and Puppet."

On the fifth day, he wasn't sure he had really come any closer to the beast, but he could see it more clearly, as if his senses were growing sharper from one day to the next: it was no longer just a shadow, it was his dog of a father, the enormous body covered in long black fur, and what he could not see he made up: the black gums and the snout, the open mouth, the tongue hanging limply in the salty water, the school of fish his dog of a father swam through, and the herrings, sardines and eels he gobbled as he flashed by. He remembered his brother telling him: "The monster, the storm, the shooting star... It was our dog of a father." He didn't believe it.

The true monster now—the two-headed entity, the child-killer, the purveyor of miracles—was him. His mother was right: the world was a cruel place. He would swallow his dog of a father whole.

On the sixth day, he wondered how long it had been since he had eaten or slept, then thought of that no more. His mother's voice lived on inside him, speaking to him tenderly as in the first days of his life, and, in the end, nothing else mattered. He thought he must look a little like her, his mother, with her hollow cheeks. He loved her more than anything, as he loved his brother.

A whole school of flying fish passed like a wave over the sailboat and all around the older brother. At dusk, a brilliant sun melted into the horizon. The older brother could hear his brother repeating: "The future is the sea, the future is the sea!" He saw him again, his too-short arms and that face of a pagan angel, his eyes so black and his laugh that taunted everything, but he knew it wasn't true, that the future was not the sea, that there was no future. Puppet turned toward him from the bow with his pale smile and told him, "Kill him, kill him, kill your dog of a father. Do it for your mother and for your brother." The older brother nodded in agreement. The red of the falling sky poured over the ocean. The dog of a father swam below. He had never seemed so close.

The seventh day seemed to last forever, a vengeful eternity, with the voices of his mother, his brother and Puppet trailing the older brother on his hunt. "I love you more than anything," his mother repeated. "Go, you do it. I can't," his brother told him. "Kill him! Kill him!" Puppet chanted. A strong wind filled the sail. The older brother had never gone so fast. At times it seemed that the wind would make him fly away. The voices of his mother, his brother and Puppet were one and the same in his head. "I need you," he told each one. He was getting closer to his dog of a father, like a whale he was going to harpoon. Seeing the older brother in the bow of his sailboat, with his cadaverous body cloaked in a primordial pelt and the puppet head like a tribal totem, someone might have thought it was a ghost ship, condemned to hunt for all of eternity. The dog of a father was there, just ahead. The older brother could see him again, hovering over him in his sleep, the big head sliding through his bedroom window or into the doghouse, drooling on him and befouling the air with his breath.

This time he had the upper hand, and he would have the last laugh. The sailboat plowed toward his dog of a father, Puppet laughing in the bow. The older brother unhooked his wooden arm, the gift from his brother, lifted it above his head in his other, good arm and pointed it toward the ocean like a harpoon. Under the blazing sun, it looked solid, a sharp weapon, forged in steel; a weapon nothing could prevent from killing.

The older brother was a warrior with a skeletal body clothed in a dry skin and old dog pelts. He breathed exhaustion, starving. His mother, his brother and Puppet spoke in his head. He was almost a dead man, the walking dead, out hunting. The sailboat was right over his dog of a father, cresting over his shadow. The wind was blowing on the older brother. The sun beat down on his head. As he had heard his brother's laugh, the older brother could hear the heartbeat of the shadow swimming under the surface, the heart of the shadow that had given him life, the shadow whose heartbeat gripped him, lodged in his stomach and his rib cage and his head, and which he wanted to spit and to vomit out. His body shook from top to bottom, covered in sweat. The older brother opened his mouth wide as if to scream as the wind screamed and he held it wide open, ready to swallow or to clamp down. He hurled his weapon and it sliced through the air. It plunged into the water, stabbing deeply into the dog of a father, and the older brother saw blood seeping in a thin black line up to the surface, and the ocean became murky, masking the shadow of the beast.

Soon, in the tumultuous black water, there was no trace of the beast's existence. And it might have been possible to believe it had never existed.

Alone on the edge of his sailboat, the older brother closed his eyes and collapsed, spent.

21

HE WAS LIVING IN A SEEMINGLY everlasting night, unsure whether he would ever wake from his slumber. Now and again, in the sky, an eye opened, and sometimes several, thousands even, a Milky Way of open eyes staring at the older brother as he slept, closing and opening again, and closing. He sailed, lying in his boat, a dilapidated shell floating idly. Sometimes he remembered the beast he and his brother had found in the marsh. He saw it swimming at the bottom of the oceans in the unending night, its broad body undulating far from the birds, mammals and insects that would dispose of it in the end.

In the sky, the eyes blinked. A shadow passed between them and the older brother's sailboat. It was his father's head, enormous and still drooling. His maw was open and thick black blood flowed out, his own blood, pouring over the body of his son, and the head opened dead eyes before fading, drowned in the dreams that would hold him forever captive.

The older brother wouldn't see it again. He would even doubt he had ever seen it. He would come to believe that they had only met as two characters in the unlikely story of an illusory life that had taken shape deep within him.

22

WHEN HE AWOKE, the older brother saw light behind his eyelids. Wood creaked, and he heard the noise of water pouring into a dish, and bed-sheets rustling, and he fell back asleep.

Later, when he opened his eyes, he noticed that he was lying on a bed, near a window through which a black raven stared at him. He was thirsty. He fell asleep again.

When he opened his eyes, the raven wasn't there anymore. The older brother was cold despite the blankets heavy on his body, and although sweat dotted his forehead. He let his eyelids drop again and soon fell into a dreamless sleep. He barely noticed someone carefully lifting his head and pouring water between his lips.

Later, he saw the raven at the window, and he wanted to talk to it as to an old friend, but when he opened his mouth, his tongue was heavy in his chalky mouth and he preferred to keep quiet, and soon fell asleep again. He thought his sleep would be dreamless again, a lifeless sleep, the sleep of death.

When he awoke the next few times, he often saw a young woman who came to give him water. On occasion, when he felt better, an old man with a white, oval face helped her, sitting him up and feeding him mash. "It's a miracle you survived," the old man murmured, and the older brother saw him smile, a friendly smile, and warm, almost surreal to him.

After a meal, his stomach gurgled, reassuring him and even making him smile. Sweet music, the music of his guts telling him that he was well and truly alive. He thought of his mother, he remembered that one day she had told him and his brother stories of a time when people spoke with their bellies, when the stomach was the seat of consciousness, and they gurgled at each other, an unearthly yet familiar language that no one could decipher anymore.

The older brother liked this idea, he found it simple and pleasing, and it reminded him of the laughter he had shared with his brother when their stomachs gurgled, like sidekicks whose bellies shared secrets more intimate still than those they whispered in each other's ears. He missed hearing his brother laugh, and laughing with him.

He slept a lot; he slept almost all the time, this boy whose life had been a waking dream and increasingly a nightmare he never thought he could escape. His eyes never stayed open for long, often only while he was being washed or fed, or when he looked out the window to see if he could see the raven.

One day, when he saw the bird looking at him, the older brother said, "You don't know everything I've lived through," and it seemed to him that the bird nodded its head. It must've seen a few things too, the bird, with its round black eye, the eye that looked like the older brother's eyes, and the younger brother's, they who had seen things, more than many men at the end of their lives.

The next day, the raven came back, and the older brother remembered the bird he had eaten raw; the taste, especially, still in his throat, and he threw up, a light, milky bile that the young girl cleaned with a warm damp towel.

He was sleeping less, and he saw the girl who was taking care of him more frequently, a fleshy girl with long black hair, but he didn't speak to her. He preferred to talk to the raven: "Did you know my brother? You've seen him. He was beautiful, with his dwarf arms. He laughed so much. In some ways, he was an angel... Were you there, that day, when he found long strands of wrack on the beach, and he wrapped the seaweed around a dead tree as if to clothe a totem pole? Do you remember the day he stomped on that big anthill? Did you ever see him chasing big black beetles between the stones, for fun, running almost on all fours, his hands flipping stones as fast as he could? One day, he painted the ones he caught: one red, one black, one gold." The older brother continued to talk about his brother; he spoke only of him, and often he thought he felt his left side tingling, a kind of tickle where his missing arm would have been.

One day, the young girl caught the older brother talking to the raven.

"Is that how it is? You talk to ravens but not to me. The villagers are right: you're a strange bird." She was nice to him, the older brother thought. She took care of him as she would have her grandfather or a newborn. He smiled at her, but didn't speak: he didn't feel like talking to her, there was nothing he would have wanted to tell her.

Little by little, the older brother slept less and ate more. The old man with the oval face came to see him more often with the young girl, and the older brother understood that he was her father. They spoke to him, telling him that the sea and the wind had pushed his boat into a bay on their island, that they had found him lying in the bottom, skeletal in his animal skins, they had rescued him, for a long time they doubted he would survive, but he had proven to be surprisingly tenacious, as if he were not destined to die.

The older brother said nothing. He didn't want to talk to them. He was surprised that his heart was still beating, that his lungs still drew air and that his digestive system still worked. It didn't make him especially happy; nor would he have preferred to die. He let himself live, sluggishly. He would have been happy just talking to the ravens, telling them everything he knew about his brother; he could've stayed in that room forever, fed by others, with no plans or ambitions, but he felt that the girl and her father had done too much for him to live, and that he owed them at least a willingness to do so. He did not wish to talk to them about his life, he didn't want to tell them anything about himself, but he didn't want to disappoint them either, as he hadn't wanted to disappoint his brother, the brother whose absence he felt again, whom he loved with all his heart, maybe more than he had ever loved, much more surely than he had loved the grey dog, much more, surely, then he had loved his mother, with more affection than he had felt for Puppet. Deep down, his brother might have been the only thing that mattered to him, the only thing that had ever counted, from the beginning.

One day, when the young girl brought him food, the older brother let his eyes drop to her chest and he felt a familiar heat spreading in his belly, but he told himself she wasn't for him: he had killed children in their beds, slain his father, and loved a dog. In the home of this young woman he was becoming a man again, but he was still possessed by the memory of his bestiality.

Finally, he had to get up and put on clean clothes, and he walked unevenly, first with the help of the young girl and her father then by himself, wobbling on his two legs.

Outside the bedroom, in the dining room, he saw his dog pelts hanging on the wall, very straight, one next to the other, proof of what he had been. The older brother ran his fingers over the fur, which was soft and smooth: the young girl had taken care to wash them.

He also saw three wooden puppets sitting on a bench: the first dressed and made up like a man, the second like a woman, and the last like a little girl; finely crafted marionettes with articulated limbs, carefully assembled.

One day, the young girl's father showed the older brother his workshop: he saw arms, legs and heads; cans of paint to outline the puppets' faces; and pine and cedar logs that would become their bodies. The older brother also saw the head of his Puppet, the black and white paint on the wooden face almost gone, and the sight of it made his stomach hurt. "I took it from your boat. It's yours," the old man said. The older brother shook his head and left the room, and he envisioned one of the old man's creations lost at sea and carried on the waves, slowly overcome by brown and green seaweed, snails and shells stuck to its body, and carried out, far out, to the brothers' childhood home, that impervious world closed in on itself where their mother would have loved to keep them, and which he longed for now. He had begun to see it again in his dreams, he and his brother running across the fields and barking like dogs, hunting moorhens, rats and lost cats, and burying their bones.

His dreams whetted something in him, and he secretly wished to find them again in his sleep, yet he avoided sleep, he slept less and less, going to bed only when he was truly exhausted, and trying as much as he could to fill his days. They were dog dreams that the older brother enjoyed guiltily. He would have liked to forget the horrors of his dog's life.

He had begun to help around the house. He carried water. He cleaned the chicken coop. One day he even took a fishing rod, sat on the end of the wharf, and he couldn't help but think of his brother, almost believing he could feel him huddled against him as on that miraculous day when they had fished the dog, and he brought his hosts a superb silvery salmon, the nicest fish he had ever caught.

He walked a lot on the island, an island of wheat fields and conifers all around the house of the young girl and her father, a house built outside the village that served as a port of call for travellers; a village the older brother avoided, since he attracted too many looks, with his one arm and his status as castaway. He preferred the solitude of the fields and the woods, the ocean wind, and the company of the ravens he continued to talk to.

The birds accompanied him every time he went out. Sometimes, one of them would even perch on his shoulder. He talked to them about his childhood, always, and his brother, but he embellished his tales, telling them the stories his mother had told him, stories in which his younger brother dug tunnels under the hill, a network of tunnels and underground rooms, a realm of wonders where the older brother and the younger had pieced together beings out of bones, phantasmagorical beasts made of animal remains, which came to life in the heart of the hill, in an eerie universe that was best avoided. That was what he told them, and many other stories, stories in which the wind always blew off the sea, stories redolent of the smell of the fields and the hills where the brothers had played as children, and sometimes a raven cawed at him in thanks.

That was the world the older brother decided to go back to.

Without him having to ask, the young girl and her father offered to help him return to the mainland, and he nodded his agreement at their proposal, a proposal with no ulterior motive—it wasn't a way to make him leave—and for which the older brother was deeply grateful, with a fond, loving gratitude he had not often felt.

One morning, they brought him to the port, he clasped them against him with his lone arm, bade them farewell, and boarded a small trade ship headed for the mainland. As his only baggage, the older brother took with him his pelt and the grey dog's, keeping them tightly rolled in a bag.

As he was about to leave, a group of ravens landed on the ship to follow him on his voyage.

That evening, wrapped up in a blanket in the bottom of the boat, he saw his mother holding a knife in the sun, she was enormously tall, her proportions legendary, and he thought that he loved her, and he saw the young girl, her white skin shining in the moonlight, and more than ever he felt the return of human desire.

PART IV

Brothers

23

HE SPOTTED A FEW HOUSES IN A VALLEY, in the middle of the fields, not far from a small fishing port with a few boats floating on the water.

Slowly he came down the hill, remembering familiar smells, the smell of the earth and the wheat; the smells of the sea too, which the wind blew against his face. A few ravens flapped their wings around him. He didn't know how long they had been with him; since his departure from the island where he had been taken in, then on the mainland where they had landed together and where they had followed the shore for a long time, walking mostly during the days, taking their time, through disparately populated landscapes, the plains and hills along the coast.

They had slept sheltered in a grove of trees or an old barn, avoiding the company of men as much as possible. In some villages, the older brother had stood in the public square, raised his arm high above his head, and spread his fingers, and the villagers had watched the ravens alight. Some offered the bird man something to eat, a pittance the stranger shared with his ravens before leaving again.

One night, they had walked around a small coastal town, the town where the older brother had lived as a pet before becoming a savage beast, a killer dog, then a fiend with two murderous heads, an inhuman creature driven by a hollow rage. He had walked around it to avoid the memory of the grey dog and because he still felt at the back of his throat an evil, vengeful anger, the desire to resume hostilities.

He had preferred to go on his way.

But that day, on the side of the hill, no bark rose up from his belly; he was at peace. He stopped and lay down in the grass. The ravens landed around him, foraging in the soil with the tips of their beaks. The older brother chewed a blade of grass. He was in no rush, he had no reason to be, he knew where he was going.

Shortly before dusk, as the fishermen were returning to the village, he got up, took his two dog pelts out of his bag, and put them on one over the other. "It's time," he told the ravens, and walked with them to the village. A group of young men and gangly teenagers sat in the square, around the grey wood table where they gathered after a day of fishing, many of them now going out with their fathers. They didn't see the older brother come up, busy laughing or telling each other about their day spent at sea or in the hills. They didn't see him come up, although he walked in the mud in the middle of the only street in the village. They only saw him when he passed them. All of them fell silent, and the one who was missing a tooth then all the others turned to him, this young man who walked slowly and confidently in his inexplicable garb, with a raven on his shoulder and others flying around him, like flies on windless summer days.

He raised his arm slightly in greeting, he turned his head toward them and they recognized him, the armless child, the old lady's son, who with his weird brother would come trade their finds, freakish insects or fossils, objects that the Great Tide had tossed on the beach. They recognized him and they were afraid, seeing the blackness of his eyes, a deep, abyssal blackness, come from the origins of the world, much darker than how they remembered him from childhood.

They let him pass without saying a word, and only when he was heading into the deepening dark, his tall, skinny body cloaked in worn animal skins, did they speak. "It's him. Did you recognize him? It's him." And the older brother laughed as his brother would have laughed; he laughed for his own pleasure and for the ravens, telling them, "You recognize them, those are the leech-boys of my childhood. And they're afraid."

24

HE WAS IN NO RUSH. That night, he slept in a hollow in the fields, with the wind blowing above him, the ravens huddled against his body, and a few nocturnal mammals—weasels, wild cats, shrews—come to see who had returned.

The next morning, he got up with the sun and headed toward the rock where he and his brother had built their bone beasts. He found the remains of Puppet, forlorn wreckage: a headless torso with two dangling legs and an arm. He also found all kinds of bones scattered over the ground, the remains of long-dead animals, nothing to do with the creatures he and his brother had imagined.

He sat in the shade with what was left of Puppet and the scattered bones. With a stone, he shattered the remaining limbs of the wooden boy, and took a leg to make a tongue protruding from the crushed skull of a dog. He inserted Puppet's torso into a cow's rib cage, as though into a suit of armour made of bone, and gave it two vertebrae as eyes, the eyes of a headless being. He went on, creating water striders, mandibular insects, huge raptors... Then he lay down in the middle of his animals and the ravens and he was happy, a pale happiness he knew was fleeting but which tasted like childhood and reminded him of his brother.

He stayed that way for a long time, letting ants crawl over his body, breathing the air, explaining to the ravens that these bone beasts were nothing compared to what his brother could have made with his own hands.

He stayed that way for a long time, sometimes feeling like he was among his own, but always with the emptiness on his left, an emptiness he had sometimes thought he could fill, but which always caught up to him.

He stayed that way for a long time, knowing he would never really be able to live without his brother.

25

THE SALT MARSH. The beach. With the long pier that still reached out, unaccountably still standing. Higher up, in the furrows of the hill, the old grey clapboard house, its walls twisted by the wind. A little farther, a wide flat stone, maybe the spot where, he told the ravens, his mother had spilled his blood to give him a brother, and on this day he was grateful to her.

The older brother walked toward the house as if in a dream. Everything was in its place, the setting almost too perfect. "Isn't it how I told you?" he repeated to the ravens. "Isn't it?" And he thought he saw them nod.

A carefree euphoria floated up from his stomach. His footsteps seemed light. He felt foolishly like skipping. He pointed out the places of his childhood, describing them to the ravens, reminding them of their history. He was happy, a somewhat suspect happiness, touched by delirium; happiness brought on by this return to the place he and his brother had so wanted to leave, toward the place they had declared dead, and which the older brother would never have believed he would see again with his own eyes.

Walking toward the house, he saw that it was overrun by thornbushes. They scratched his legs and his hand bled when he brushed them away. There were no more goats in the pen, only a bony carcass long since picked clean by scavengers.

A few steps away from the house, he saw a grey fieldmouse slipping under the door. The older brother stayed frozen in front of the door, hesitating, then pushed it open, nervously. A kind of irresistible foreboding drew him forward. He walked through the dust and the carcasses of insects, their chitinous bodies cracking underfoot. The ravens followed in a slow procession.

Light poured into the room behind him, and filtered weakly through the filthy windows. He

144

saw something move by the hearth, an unnatural horned animal huddled in the shadows. Moving closer, he realized it was a goat, a goat that looked like it might have been centuries old, its hair heavy with dust falling in clumps to the floor, dry teats hanging flaccidly, and the long, venerable horns, their innumerable notches counting the years. It was a creature he and his brother might have invented, but today it was the last living companion of his decrepit mother, who was sitting at the dining room table, tiny, her body horribly puckered; she was almost mummified, barely more living than dead, the embodiment of drought sitting before her plate as if at a meal.

The table was set for her and her two sons. The older brother approached and sat in his spot without his mother noticing. She spoke to him in a weak, hoarse voice, arid, as if she had been talking to him since his departure. For her, he had never left. "Go catch some crabs," she told him. "You should go crabbing more often. I prefer goat meat, but we have to keep some for winter. You've noticed, the days are getting shorter... The summer's almost over." And she spoke also to his brother, who she thought still sat at the same table. "You'll go too, won't you?

You'll go crabbing with your brother. Or gather some shells. But don't come home too late. You always come home too late."

The older brother closed his eyes, breathed in, and thought he smelled his mother's goat stew, and the smell of her seaweed tea and boiled milk, and he thought he heard his brother stirring on the bench next to him, as he had squirmed as a child, always impatient to leave the table to run outside and see what marvels the ocean might have left on the beach: the body of a sea otter, maybe, or a barrel full of sticky black goo.

It occurred to him that he was going to take care of his mother, that he would have her all to himself and they would live together, in their own world, with the ghost of his brother, lulled by the raspy bleating of the immortal goat, but he knew he had never really believed that. His mother had not needed him for a long time. He had not come back for her: he had always only been looking for his brother.

Again he imagined his brother next to him, close, on his left side—his breath on his skin— and he thought he heard him say: "You abandoned me." The older brother inhaled and saw again the black ocean, sinister shadows swimming under the surface. He remembered the heat and the thirst, the salt water on his skin, the immeasurable fatigue. He felt the emptiness to his left, the absence that had been with him since the day of his birth. He nodded to his brother: "Yes, I abandoned you." But he also remembered that he had killed the one who was the cause of their misery, and he wanted to cry great heaving sobs, release all the love and all the disgust of his life.

He remembered the violence, the savage vengefulness he had aroused within himself. He envisioned himself slitting the throat of his old mother and her goat, mixing their blood on the ground in the dust, the alphabet of the apocalypse, the language of disaster, senseless. He saw it as he had pictured so many stories, a story he might have told the ravens. He saw it as he got up and walked out, leaving the door open behind him. The ravens followed. He walked slowly to the sea, stumbling like a useless god, unknown to all and ineffectual. He took off his mud-spattered boots, removed his pelts and let them fall behind him. He was naked, his body skinny, and he could almost feel the wind blowing between his vertebrae. The ravens were still with him, some of them cawing. He walked out onto the pier, crushing the shells of long-dead molluscs and crustaceans, his bare feet sinking here and there between the rotting boards.

He walked out to the end of the pier, before the immense sea. The black water lapped at his feet. The sky weighed down on his skull. In the distance, a cormorant called. He imagined he had a knife in his hand, the same one his mother had used on the day of his birth, lifting his arm to drive the blade into his shoulder, and he screamed in pain as he had on the first day of his life. And he slowly cut his arm, his only arm, an atrocious act of self-mutilation that would bring his brother back to life.

He imagined it, but did nothing.

The waves crashed on the rocks. In the distance, the older brother thought he saw his brother swimming. He thought he saw him, but he knew it wasn't him, only the reflection of the moon, maybe, or the last rattle of a hallucinated life.

His gaze was lost over the endless sea, an uncharted world, impossible to fathom, and he wondered where the island was where he had been taken in by the young girl and her father.

A raven landed on his shoulder, and he murmured, "Brother, everything here is dead: I'm going back out to sea."

QC Fiction brings you the very best of a new generation of Quebec storytellers, sharing surprising, interesting novels in flawless English translation.

Available from QC Fiction:

LIFE IN THE COURT OF MATANE by Eric Dupont
(translated by Peter McCambridge)

THE UNKNOWN HUNTSMAN by Jean-Michel Fortier
(translated by Katherine Hastings)

BROTHERS by David Clerson
(translated by Katia Grubisic)

Coming soon from QC Fiction:

LISTENING FOR JUPITER by Pierre-Luc Landry
(translated by Arielle Aaronson and Madeleine Stratford)

BEHIND THE EYES WE MEET by Mélissa Verreault
(translated by Arielle Aaronson)

Visit **qcfiction.com** for details and to subscribe
to a full season of QC Fiction titles.

RECYCLED
Paper made from
recycled material
FSC
www.fsc.org   FSC® C100212

Printed in October 2016
by Gauvin Press,
Gatineau, Québec